Dear Parents,

Welcome to the Scholastic Reader series. We have taken over 80 years of experience with teachers, parents, and children and put it into a program that is designed to match your child's interests and skills.

Level 1—Short sentences and stories made up of words kids can sound out using their phonics skills and words that are important to remember.

Level 2—Longer sentences and stories with words kids need to know and new "big" words that they will want to know.

Level 3—From sentences to paragraphs to longer stories, these books have large "chunks" of texts and are made up of a rich vocabulary.

Level 4—First chapter books with more words and fewer pictures.

It is important that children learn to read well enough to succeed in school and beyond. Here are ideas for reading this book with your child:

- Look at the book together. Encourage your child to read the title and make a prediction about the story.
- Read the book together. Encourage your child to sound out words when appropriate. When your child struggles, you can help by providing the word.
- Encourage your child to retell the story. This is a great way to check for comprehension.
- Have your child take the fluency test on the last page to check progress.

Scholastic Readers are designed to support your child's efforts to learn how to read at every age and every stage. Enjoy helping your child learn to read and love to read.

—Francie Alexander
Chief Education Officer
Scholastic Education

Text copyright © 2000 by Hans Wilhelm, Inc.
Activities copyright © 2003 Scholastic Inc.

Library of Congress Cataloging-in-Publication Data is available.

ISBN 0-439-19288-9

10   07

Printed in the U.S.A.   23
First printing, September 2000

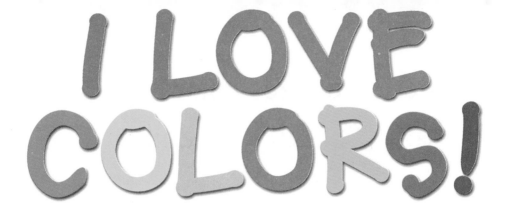

I LOVE COLORS!

by **Hans Wilhelm**

Scholastic Reader — Level 1

SCHOLASTIC INC. Cartwheel ·B·O·O·K·S· ®

New York Toronto London Auckland Sydney
Mexico City New Delhi Hong Kong Buenos Aires

There are three colors:
RED, **YELLOW**, and **BLUE**.

I will make a picture.

I can use my tail
as a brush.

Oooops!

This looks good!

I will do some more.

Now I have three colors:
RED, **ORANGE**,
and **YELLOW**.

RED mixed with **YELLOW** makes **ORANGE**.

My feet are still white....

Now they are BLUE!

What will happen when
I dip my YELLOW feet
into BLUE?

They turn GREEN!
YELLOW mixed with BLUE
makes GREEN.

And now I will dip my
RED tail into **BLUE**.
What will happen?

It turns **PURPLE**!
RED mixed with **BLUE**
makes **PURPLE**.

Uh, oh! The paint is
getting sticky and stiff!

Watch out!
Here comes **RAINBOW** Dog!

Splash!!!

Now I'm myself again.

But maybe I should keep
a little bit of color.
What do you think?